WAKING DREAMS

SHORT STORIES
BY NEERJA K

Edited by

Juhi Kalia

INDIA • SINGAPORE • MALAYSIA

ISBN

Hardcase 979-8-89277-807-7
Paperback 979-8-89233-774-8

Cover By Juhi Kalia

About the Author

Neerja: A writer, producer, director, songwriter, artist, and philanthropist, Neerja wears many hats with ease. She is an army wife and a mother of two. She was born in Srinagar and comes from a talented family of creators and broadcast pioneers. As an artist her evocative landscapes of Kashmir have been featured at multiple exhibitions and most recently at The India Habitat Centre. Neerja writes best at Colonel's Cottage, her retreat in the Sahyadries.

From the adventures of charmed childhood in her Nonie series to the rousing stories in Fauji Heart, her writing draws deeply from the well of an eventful life, a rich imagination, and a tender heart.

This collection of eleven short stories is her most personal work yet. Sometimes dark and wicked, these tales full of twists, turns, death, romance, and the afterlife will leave you with more questions than answers.

You can visit her Instagram Handle at… Neerja Kalia.

Disclaimer

This is a work of fiction. Names, characters, places, events and incidents are the products of the author's imagination. Any resemblance to actual persons, living or dead, or actual events is purely coincidental.

I love these lines from a John T Graham's song.

'Today not tomorrow,
There is no time to borrow,
Today is a good day to live,
Today not tomorrow.'

Dedication

This book is dedicated to my grandchildren, Agastyaa and Chaitanya. They keep me alive and excited. May we continue to grow, explore and learn life's lessons from one another.

Thank you, Agastyaa, for listening to these stories and giving me your insightful feedback at every stage of my initial drafts.

Thank you Juhi, for editing and polishing these stories, so they may shine brighter.

And ever present gratitude to Neha, Priya and Sanjala for always encouraging me and believing in me.

Contents

Midnight Guest

It must have been shortly after midnight but the darkness these days was so dark, it felt like it was much later. Martin was lying down, hoping for some rest. His quarters were cramped but comfortable. He whispered his prayers and had just closed his eyes when he heard someone sobbing. He listened intently but it stopped. It was probably just some drunk, maudlin man on the street outside stumbling home from the pub. He closed his eyes and started to drift off but then he heard it again. It was coming from right next door. The poor, wretched man sounded terribly distraught. He sobbed and sniffed while muttering and cursing under his breath. Martin couldn't make out exactly what he was saying. But it was loud enough to keep him up. And it got louder and louder. He could not see him but he could hear how much crushing despair this man was in – the kind of howls and wails that come only from a deep dark devastated place inside your soul.

He waited patiently for a pause in the anguish. Should he say something? But then he would know he had heard him. He felt burdened like an awkward stranger intruding on an intensely private breakdown.

"Uh...hey, are you ok? Do you need any help?"

The crying stopped abruptly. And then after a long pause, the voice spoke "Sorry, who's there? Are you next door?"

"Yes, I suppose, we're neighbours," said Martin. I didn't realize the place was occupied. I've never heard anyone before."

"I just got here today," replied the man, his voice hoarse from all the crying. "Sorry, if I woke you. I know it's late. I'll be quiet."

"No no, it's all right. I was awake anyway. It's not your fault. The sound really carries at night here," said Martin.

"Sure does," agreed the voice.

Martin didn't want to pry but there was something about his voice...also if he was being honest, he had been pretty lonely out here. It was nice to have someone to talk to. He cleared his throat and tried to make small talk.

"So you got in this evening? From where abouts?"

"Oh, it's a long terrible story. Not sure you'll want to get to know me after you hear it."

"I've got no place to go. Not tonight anyway," said Martin. "I'm supposed to head out soon but I'm waiting for something first. So go on…I won't judge, you know what they say – sharing your secrets lightens your burdens."

The new neighbor sighed heavily and said, "I was in prison up North. They put me in solitary and then they moved me here this morning."

Martin was now wide awake, "For real? What did you do?"

There was a long pause. Martin thought he'd scared him off with his eagerness and curiosity.

But then he heard him scoff… "Have you ever been to prison, neighbour? Not your local lockup but a proper penitentiary? Straight-up, solitary confinement for days with only a hole in the floor to crap in and no light, no air? It all blurs. Your mind starts playing tricks on you. You breathe in the same air you just breathed out. And it's cold, so miserable and cold. You can't even stretch your legs when you sleep, makes this place seem like the Ritz."

"I'm sorry, that sounds awful," said Martin.

Drenched in self-loathing, the voice spoke sharply this time, "Oh, don't go feeling sorry for me. I don't deserve your kindness or sympathy. I am a horrible human being. I've done such despicable shameful things."

Martin sensed this was getting dark and suddenly he wished he'd just kept quiet and gone to sleep. But it would be rude now, to leave this conversation so he said, "You don't have to tell me if you don't feel comfortable, you know."

But his new neighbor kept talking like a runaway train now, "I haven't slept in days you know. Even though it was dark in solitary, I'd be wide awake thinking and reliving it all and staring into the abyss. No sweet sleep for me. I'm cursed now. I wish I could go back and undo it all. Start over. Oh, what a fool I was. So greedy and wicked and easily corruptible, that was me. All she had to do was glance at me across the room, in that secret coy way she had and I was ready to die for her. More like kill for her, I suppose. Sorry, look at me even now! I'm the worst. Keeping you up with my troubles. All me me me! Free therapy in the middle of the night from such a kind man as yourself. Enough about me. How long have you been here? You mentioned you might be leaving soon?"

"I've been here a while," said Martin.

"Do you like it here?"

"What kind of question is that? What sane person would want to be here willingly? I'm just waiting to tie up a few loose ends and then I'll be off. Hopefully to someplace less cold and dreary. So this woman, what was her name? Tell me more, won't you? What did you do? Why were you uhm…upset earlier?"

"Why does it matter? It's all sickening and depraved. I don't want to ruin your night."

Martin said, "Oh please, you may as well talk to me while I'm still here. And don't worry, I am not easily distressed. You have no idea what I have gone through in my life. Nothing can shock me anymore. So, go on…"

After a heavy sigh, the new neighbor spoke, "It's so easy to blame it all on her. Was she wily and beautiful and cunning? Yes, but I was the idiot. I am the one who made all the wrong choices. It felt so alive, the trespassing and the secrets and the stolen kisses. It's like I was high all the time. I couldn't think straight through the fog of heady desire. She told me he was cruel. And I believed her. How could I? I'd known him since we were kids running around in the woods. He wouldn't hurt a fly. So how did I believe that he could beat her? But she showed me these bruises. Oh, she was so good. Leading me on. Playing the victim, promising me the moon and the stars and a lifetime of those legs and that wild hair…but suddenly so virginal and dignified in court. She was so good as the grieving young widow, even I was convinced."

His voice became heavy with grief and he started weeping again, inconsolable, out of control weeping!

Martin let him cry. Then in a trembling voice, he continued, "I should have spoken to him. But instead, I killed him. He was my best friend. We were like brothers. And I betrayed him. I murdered him in cold blood. Sure, she played games and made me doubt him.

Planting little seeds of hate and jealousy and anger till it all boiled over but like I said, she didn't do the murdering. *I* did.

I am the one whose wretched hands picked up a rock and bashed his poor head in, with that rock. So I am the one who will rot in hell. I am the one who shall never be forgiven. I am a monster. Oh my God, I can still see the look in his eyes. I'm sorry, I'm sorry, I'm so sorry…" he howled in agony.

Martin felt the open bloody gash on his forehead, he felt no pain. He felt nothing anymore. Tears rolled down his cheeks in dirty streaks as he spoke now, "Bobby, it's ok my friend. I've been waiting for so long to hear you say this. Now I can go in peace. I had a feeling it was you. When they put you in the ground next to me this morning, I wasn't sure… but I wanted to know the truth from you."

Bobby's words came out in a jumbled stream of shock and emotion, "Martin! I'm sorry Martin. Oh God, Martin, I deserve to die and suffer for what I did to you."

Martin laughed wryly and said, "Well you can't die twice my friend. I watched your burial…and I heard your suffering."

"I got what I deserved," Bobby said, "justice is.."

"No Bobby," Martin cut him off, "this is not justice. She's still out there alive and well, enjoying her freedom and my money. And look at us? Two fools lying in their graves."

"Martin, does your head still hurt?" asked Bobby.

There was no answer. Only silence. Silence of death.

* * * * * * *

The Pact

Sehar found herself walking through a sublime valley. The river below was slow-moving and calm, much like the throng of people around her, all unhurriedly snaking their way up the mountain path. Everyone seemed to be mesmerized by the view - the lofty snow-clad mountains standing majestically against the cerulean sky, the low-hanging puffs of lazy clouds weaving in and out of the peaks, the fields upon fields of daffodils skirting both the banks of the river and the enormous orchids gracefully swaying from the trees…it was breathtaking. We've all had moments like this, haven't we? When you feel, at one with the universe. So overwhelmed by the beauty that you need to share it with someone you love or you'll just die.

She turned to Uday, excitedly, thinking, 'Look at the light dancing in the clouds, can you see it?' She wanted to squeeze his hand. But wait, how strange, she couldn't feel his hand in hers. She looked down, turned back, and looked all around in the crowd. Where was he? Wasn't he right here by her side just a moment ago? She stood up on her toes and tried to look over the sea of heads bobbing ahead. He had this awful habit of walking too fast as though he was perpetually late for something. She had protested all her life about how she couldn't keep up. But this was different; she recalled very clearly, that they had left together hand in hand. But now, there was no sign of him. Had he stopped for something? Had she left him behind? She stopped unsure of whether to walk ahead or turn back.

She scanned the crowd for his warm brown eyes and his generous smile. Uday, where the hell are you? So many faces, from so many parts of the world! Men and women, old and young, and some children too. This had happened once before in the Grand Bazaar when they had snuck out on a secret holiday. They had got separated in the Warrens when she had stopped to window shop. But he'd found her easily. How upset he had been with her! But now Saher worried. There were too many people. It looked like everyone had heard about the view. Perhaps they should have picked a less popular spot. Udaaaay…? Where are you? Her hands instinctively went to her pockets, searching for her phone. Where had she kept it?

She felt a surge of anger. How could he be so careless? But then it passed and she just felt anxious. What if he was hurt? Had he fallen? I hope he's all right, she silently prayed. She dropped her speed to a snail's pace, letting everyone overtake her. No sign of him. She took a deep breath and reassured herself. They would find each other, eventually. After all, Uday would also be looking for her. Soon she was the last person walking at the end. The stragglers also disappeared over the hill and now she found herself walking alone. The light was starting to fade. Her heart sank along with the sun. The crowd had been swallowed by the mist that was rising from the river and getting denser by the minute.

In the distance, she saw the faint outline of a long bridge that got lost at the other end. So it seemed. The people now looked like stick figures, they were so far ahead. Many of them were now crossing the bridge.

What should she do? Should she keep waiting here for Uday or should she run and catch up with the throng, just in case he was already up ahead? Classic Uday, ruining this perfect moment with all this stress and drama, she thought with a wry smile. She was going to be so mad at him when she found him. The river had gone from a dreamy powder blue to a golden lavender as the setting sun danced on the water. The mist rose from its surface like a muslin wrap, trying to engulf the whole place. She kept walking…

Her heart pined for Uday. She was sure, that at any moment he would come running from behind and startle her with a big yell and a laugh and she would yell at him and smack him and they would both laugh at the whole thing, walking hand in hand. After all, wasn't it this, what they had both wanted for so long? To be together in a beautiful place like this. Everything was perfect, peaceful, and serene. Except, Uday wasn't here. The nagging worry was back. Where was he? It was getting late. This wasn't funny anymore. Her mind started imagining the worst - Uday lying trampled and hurt and alone on the rocks or by the river. Had he fallen? Udaaaaaay! Udaaaaaaaaay! She called out in desperation.

Immersed in her troubling thoughts she did not realize she was already at the bridge now.

Through the mist, she discerned a figure walking towards her. Could it be him? Alas, it was a woman. She had a kind face and a notepad in her hand. Maybe there was a toll for the bridge. Where was her wallet? Uday always kept tickets and cash in his. He was way more responsible than her with that kind of stuff.

"Sehar, there you are!" said the woman as she walked toward her. Sehar froze in fear and confusion. Who was she? How did she know her name? Of course, silly me, she would have my name on the list of today's bookings. In fact, she might be able to find Uday for me!

"Why have you stopped Saher? You must cross the bridge now! What are you waiting for? It's getting very late. We need to hurry. Come with me; let's mark your entry in the list."

Saher exclaimed, "But I can't, not yet! Have you seen Uday? Maybe he's gone ahead and we've somehow missed each other. I mean my…uhm …have you seen a man coming through? 5'8, curly hair, he's in a pink shirt?" The woman looked down at her list. Saher kept muttering, "No, he's probably just running late. As usual." She smiled indulgently. "I'll wait for him here if you don't mind and then we will cross the bridge together, I can't leave him behind."

"Leave who behind? There is no one else scheduled to arrive today, you are the last one", said the woman in a kindly voice. "What's the name you said?" "Uday?" She took a little longer this time looking at her notes. She shook her head, "I'm afraid that name isn't here in my records."

"Please check again, there must be some mistake. We left together. He was just with me before we lost each other in the crowd," Sehar pleaded.

The woman looked intrigued, "That is impossible. We have never made a mistake like this before. Let me check again."

Sehar squeezed her eyes shut and prayed hard for Uday's name to be there.

The woman touched Sehar's shoulder and gently asked, "Who is this Uday, Sehar? And why do you believe that he should be here with you?" Sehar opened her eyes, blinking back tears, "Uday?! How do I begin to tell you who he is to me? Uday is my life. My soul mate. We grew up together in the same little neighbourhood. Our houses were so close, yet so far apart. Each side of the street prayed to their own God. And their hate was so strong it wouldn't let our love live. There was no question of talking it out. The poison of fear and rage had festered for so many generations, they were blind. We decided to elope but there was no place to hide. We knew that they would hunt us down and kill both of us. My father and two brothers would surely kill Uday first and then me."

"We tried to forget each other but it was impossible. In the end, we made a pact together. We decided to take a step that would liberate us from the shackles of our religion and community. We could be free and together forever. Ultimately we decided to go where no one could find us." The woman interrupted, "So you chose to come here! Let me see if I can find your Uday." She closed her eyes and focused. Then she beckoned for Saher to come closer. An image appeared in the mist. Saher stretched out her hand longing to touch Uday, "Yes, that's him!" she said, bursting with joy. Then she saw herself beside him and it slowly started to come back. This exact moment replayed in slow agony.

Her smile faded as she watched and remembered what had happened. Tears started rolling down her cheeks.

"Should I stop it?" the woman asked.

Sehar shook her head and watched transfixed, wishing she could change it.

Sehar and Uday were standing together in a tight embrace on the terrace of a high-rise building. A full moon shone bright and the clear sky was sprinkled with stars. It was a spellbinding scene if you didn't know any better. Star crossed lovers on a balmy beautiful night. More romantic than any scene in a movie. Then they disentangled themselves, looked wistfully at each other for a long moment, and then holding hands they quietly started to walk toward the far end of the terrace. Now they were both standing on the edge of the ledge. It looked like they were both going to jump together. But something flickered across Uday's face. He looked at her with love in his eyes and then at the sheer fall. The doubt stopped his feet and he started to pull her back…"No Sehar. Wait! We can't do this…I can't be the reason you die, no, wait"…but Sehar's foot was already treading air.

Uday pulled with all his might, he teetered on the edge and pulled hard, trying to somehow heave her back but it was too late. His words got drowned in his screams as Sehar's hand slipped from his and she went over the ledge. Suddenly his screams went dry in his throat and he stood there like a statue, shocked at what he had let happen. He could see Sehar, the love of his life falling down the twenty floors. Hysterical, he started pulling his hair out; he could not find his voice to scream, he started hitting his own face, his knees gave way and he sank down to the floor of the ledge. He sat there motionless, hugging both his knees, curled into a ball like a fetus.

Tears streamed down Sehar's face as she watched their separation. Her mind now remembered it all but her voice kept denying it. "No,no,no…this can't be true. Nooooo, we jumped together…we were supposed to"… the rest of her words were lost in defeated weeping as she too collapsed to the ground. Rocking herself back and forth, she cried for what seemed like a long time.

Finally, the woman spoke tenderly, "You won't find Uday here because he is not here." Sehar suddenly looked up, her voice heavy with worry, she exclaimed, "They will blame him and arrest him for my murder. How can I save him? Please you can help, tell them that it was not his fault." She pleaded. "Sehar, that is not your responsibility. It is his. He has to fight for his innocence. That is his journey and this is yours. You have come here alone and you will have to cross over now with me." Sehar was in shock. She wanted to die...but how can you die twice?

* * * * * * * *

Just Let Me Be

How peaceful is it in here! Total bliss. I am so free...free from all the worlds. Free to be ME.... just ME. There is no one to judge me, no one to rate me, no one to grade me, no one to please, no one to fear, no one to share, no one to care. No pain, no hurt, no love, no hate, no challenges, no wins no defeats. No rules no regulations, no expectations, and no duties therefore no good deeds no bad and no rewards no punishments.

I take what I need, never more, never less. I get what I want without any questions asked and with no sanctions needed. I sway freely with the tide. How wonderful it is being here! How beautiful is it? Just being! No stress no worries and no needs that are not fulfilled.

This was then but not anymore. Something started to change. No, don't get me wrong. I still get what I need but something has changed within me. I have no idea what went wrong. I still like it here but it has become a little uncomfortable. You know a little cramped. I can't move around so freely now. There was no one around but now I can hear some muffled voices. Though some of them are soothing, most are disturbing.....nasty, and loud. My ears hurt and I have to shut my eyes tighter than ever to cut the noise. The noise is simply unbearable at times. Though I get what I need, it just seems I need more and more and this place is getting smaller and smaller but I still love it in here.

Hey, who is nudging me? Please don't disturb me. I need to sleep for a while. Someone whispered, 'No. Don't sleep. Wake up. The time has come.' 'What time? And who are you to order me around? Anyway, I can't even see you?' 'Of course, you can't see me. I don't have a form. I am only a voice. I am here only to give the message that the time has come.' 'Stop!!! Stop talking to me. I don't want to be disturbed. And what are you harping about 'Time?' I don't even understand the meaning of this word! So please let me be. It is simply blissful here.' 'We could have been blissful forever you know....Nirvana....but we chose this journey together. Now get ready to tread these paths.' 'Hold on for a minute. You said 'we' what do you mean we? There is no we, there is only me.' 'No dear there is 'we'... you and me. Now stop wasting time and get ready.' 'Ready for what?' 'For a journey that is waiting for you and me.'

I just don't understand what this guy is talking about. Hey, now I can feel somebody pushing me out of my space… from my very own space. Can you imagine? Is there no justice?

The force of the push has increased and I feel suffocated. How did this place suddenly get so small? I better help myself and move out before I choke.

As I struggle out of here, I can hear some voices … happy ones but not the one I was conversing with earlier. I wonder where that voice has disappeared. I kind of feel lonely without that friendly voice. All of a sudden my space seems to have become vast and I can move and stretch my limbs again. Thank God! Why is someone holding me by my feet and …… Ouch, why the hell is someone hitting me on my bums? As I winced, the voice spoke again to me, this time with urgency, 'Hey! Stop wincing and cry out and breathe!!' 'Why?' 'You fool! I can be you, only if I enter your body….hurry up breathe!! I am your soul. I have to dwell in you.' While this conversation was on, the slaps on my bum got sharper. I yelled and my soul and I became one. They wiped my eyes open and I laid my gaze on the face of the person that had held me in her womb for nine months and now she held me in her arms….the most comforting wrap around my body and soul…..my mother's arms.

****

Maya's Blind Date

Maya dragged her unwilling heavy feet towards her home. She was sad that the work days at the office seemed to go by fast. She was happy to be in the office. These days she didn't want to go home. There was no one waiting for her there. It was a large empty house and not a home anymore. She did not want to enter that house without the aroma of the lovely cakes baking in the kitchen, her granny fussing over her snack and eagerly wanting to know everything that had happened at her office. On other days, she would be met with a cold sprinkler that Granny would suddenly point towards her while watering those beautiful hydrangeas and their laughter would echo through the sprawling garden. Granny would say cheerfully, 'Tomorrow is Sunday. Let's cycle down to the lake for a quiet picnic. I love to read my book sprawled on the grass by the lake under that weeping willow. What do you say?'

Now there is no Granny. She also left her like her parents did over two decades back. Maya was just four years old then.

Maya...... what a beautiful name it was that her grandmother had given her when she was born. It sounded so soft and musical...Maya.....felt so mystic and sweet to the ears. She too had loved her name during her growing years. However, she had never bothered to ask for its meaning from her grandmother and now she can't. A wave of nausea rose within her and along with that the shadow of sadness and loneliness engulfed her. She could barely manage to keep her steps straight. It's been a month since Granny had quietly passed on in her sleep. Maya had felt cheated. How could she go, just like that, without saying a goodbye or without giving her a last hug? Maya was shattered. She had not known life without Granny.

Maya had been her grandmother's treasure and the only reason for her to keep on living. Despite her own grief of having lost her husband at a young age and then her son and daughter-in-law, she succeeded in keeping the vibes positive and happy for this little gem of hers. Maya had missed her parents. Not that she had had any special time with them; still she felt their absence from time to time. Other than that she had had a very happy and protected childhood, a little over-protected if I may say so.

Maya entered the gate and walked into a lonely house. Even after a month, Maya felt the grief and pain of Granny's passing away as intensely as on the first day.

A good part of her had died with Granny. She hated to be alone and yet she did not meet whatever few friends she had. Her phone kept ringing but she did not feel like answering. Some friends at the office kept trying to invite her out but she declined. Now they had stopped the invitations and the phone rang lesser and lesser.

Sundays and holidays were the worst. She kept lying in bed the whole day long. There was no zing left in the holidays because there was no Granny.

Days went well with her work and office but evenings were heavy and lonely in that huge house. Granny had taught her well, how to be emotionally independent and not count on crutches from others for her own happiness and contentment. Most probably she had tried to prepare her for this situation from her childhood. They had had lot of fun together. They would watch TV, surf the net, and play pictionary, chess, and other board games. For outdoor activities, they had a badminton court in one area of their garden. They even had a basketball loop fixed on one of the garage walls. Maya was amazed at her grandmother's youthful attitude.

In the quest to make Maya strong and independent, both professionally and emotionally, Granny had gone a bit too far. She had realized that Maya had become kind of a recluse and a little, should I say, antisocial, maybe. But it was too late for Granny to make amends and life also didn't permit her to mend what was torn.

Maya felt restless in the evenings in that lonely house without Granny.

Her idol mind was wandering all over the place and suddenly it found an occupation to busy itself.... Maya! What is the meaning of Maya? She wondered.

So, she went to the only one left who could give her the answers...that was, Google. What she found there added to her confusion. This is what she found... 'Maya is a female name in many parts of the world with different meanings in different languages and cultures. Maya means illusion or magic in Sanskrit and is also an alternate name for Goddess of wealth, Lakshmi. In the Tupi language of southern Brazil, it means mother. In the Maori language of the indigenous people of New Zealand, it means courage or bravery. She learned that many Maori girls were named Maya. In Greek mythology spelt as *Maia* is the name of the mother of Hemes, son of Zeus, and means to nurture.'

Maya got herself a large cup of coffee and sat on the windowsill of one of the many bay windows in the living room. Sitting with her feet tucked under her, she let her eyes soak in the evening mist that was gradually taking the entire garden into its folds.

Maya for a moment threw her shroud of grief and loneliness away and wondered, so, what should she think her name means out of all the definitions she had just Googled. She decided that she would like to be Maya....the illusion or magic and also Maya the courage. That sounds like me, she thought... magically mystic with loads of courage. Yes, that's what my name means. She decided and felt her spirits rise a bit.

Yes, she was, courageous but it was the loneliness and the absence of Granny that she could not handle. The little pep and the courage she had felt a fraction of a second back went out of her being, 'poof!' and left her deflated like a pricked balloon.

How she wished she had some company, any company, even a dog, maybe.

Yes, that's what she should do; get a puppy for herself. But who would look after it? The housekeeper could? She was toying with the idea when her laptop chimed.

Curious, she walked over to the dining table where her laptop lay open. She saw something had popped up. It was the link to a dating app. Is this a sign? A sign from Granny? She wondered. She convinced herself that it was.

Maya wondered and smiled sadly at the large portrait of Granny that was up on the wall, right in front of her. She felt Granny was nudging her, 'Let's see what comes of it. Go ahead, click on that link.'

She sat down and clicked on the link just out of curiosity. She was amused at her thoughtlessness. She had never indulged in these apps. What prompted her to do this today? She wondered why, she had even filled in all her personal data. The index finger of her right hand seemed to have developed a will of its own and it went and clicked the OK key. There, that was not so difficult! Her index finger seemed to comment. No, but it was indeed madness. Have I gone crazy? I am talking to my own finger. She quickly hid her finger in her fist and went back to the window sill, feeling silly and sad again.

The rest of the evening melted away into the night, uneventfully. Savitri came in and said, "Deedi, shall I serve you dinner?" "I am not hungry but then I don't want to keep you. Just give me a little *daal chawal* in a thali and leave it on the dining table. You can then go to your quarters. I will eat in a while." "Maya Baby, how long are you going to be like this? You must come back towards life again. That's what Granny would want you to do. You must eat and sleep on time. I am worried about you." Saying this, Savitri went to the kitchen. She returned sooner than Maya had expected. She had brought her a *thali* full of steaming *daal chawal* and her favourite *bhindi* fry. Savitri had decided not to get bullied by Maya anymore. "Here, I have got you your *thali* but I am not going to put it on the table. You can sit where you are and have this hot food. It will do you good. No…no don't send me away. I won't go unless you start eating."

Maya gave up; she got up listlessly, washed her hands, and sat down back on the window sill.

A little chill had set in. Savitri brought her a wrap and put it around her shoulders. She snuggled into it and said, "Thank you, Savitri Deedi. Now you can go."

Maya started to eat her food as Savitri walked out. She was surprised at being suddenly hungry. So she finished every bit of the food on her *thali*.

She left the *thali* that was wiped clean, on the table, washed her hands, and came back to sit on the window sill to wallow a little more in her own pain. She rested her restless head back against the cushion and stared into the darkness outside. Savitri was right. The food in her belly did her good. Soon her eyes felt droopy and before she could even think of moving to her bedroom she dosed off into an intoxicating sleep.

She heard a soft tingling of a bell in her dream. She smiled. 'It must be Granny trying to wake me up. She uses all kinds of tricks to steal my sleep away,' went her sleepy thoughts. The tingling now turned into a loud ping, ping, ping! She opened her sleep-laden eyelids. Finding her bearings, she looked around and realized that she had fallen off to sleep, sitting on the window sill. She squinted and rubbed her eyes lazily. She looked around for the source of the sound. It was her laptop that was still open on the dining table, pinging away.

She waded to the table and sat down in front of her laptop. To her amazement, she saw her chat box with a bunch of messages and that was the explanation of the continuous pinging sound.

Who could it be?

In utter disgust, she sat down and typed, 'Who is this?'

Pat came the reply, 'A decent guy.' And a string of messages started to and fro. 'Which decent guy is up at this hour messaging a stranger?' 'Remember the dating App?' 'Oh, that was just a mistake. By the way, I should not be chatting with a total stranger.' 'I am not a stranger. I know everything about you.' 'Big deal! All my information is on the App.' 'Yes, all that and also what is not declared there. I know how lonely you have been lately after Granny passed on.' 'Wait a minute. How do you know all this? Do I know you?' 'I know you. You don't know me.' 'So, what is your name? Who are you? Introduce yourself.'

'I would rather do that in person.' 'What makes you so confident that I would want to meet you?' 'You want to lay a bet that you will come out to meet me right now?' 'That's not going to happen. I don't even know your name, and what makes you think that I'll come out to meet you at this hour? I am getting off this chat and please don't message again.' 'Try.' 'You won't close this chat box when I tell you that I am standing right outside on your porch.' 'What! That can't be true! You must be out of your mind.' 'Check it out. All you have to do is just come out.'

Maya's heart was racing now. She thought her breathing would stop any minute. She was sure she was going to get a panic attack. Anger replaced anxiety as logic took over. She grabbed her wrap and rushed out of the room barefoot. She realized that she was actually running through the corridor. She stopped near the hat rack where she always hung her work bag. She rummaged through her bag and found the pepper spray that Granny had insisted that she carry with her all the time. Now was the time to use it. That gave her a little more confidence; she quickly flung the main door open. It opened onto the porch. She came to a sudden halt and stood there in shock. She became motionless, she looked like a lifeless, beautiful painting, framed by the carved door frame.

A few feet away from her stood the most handsome man she had ever set her eyes upon. He stood there leaning against the pillar, one hand in his trouser pocket and the other supporting his jacket that was thrown casually over his shoulder. He stared at her with those flirtatious eyes. A defiant smile that lightly played on his lips made him look devastatingly attractive.

He said, "I told you that you would come out running to meet me." Maya was stunned. For a moment she was speechless and then she felt a rage consuming her, "Who the hell are you and how can you come to my doorstep without my permission, and that too in the middle of the night?" Though her tone was authoritative, there was an undercurrent of a shiver in her voice, "You ask too many questions. First of all, put that pepper spray away. You won't need it, I assure you." He said in a calming voice. "Come let's sit for a while and enjoy life in this beautiful moment. Who knows what comes next!" Maya was astonished at the ease with which he was hijacking the conversation, "You know, that I am not alone here, I just have to call out and my caretakers will be here and they will throw you out. Just a minute, how the hell did you come in? There is a padlock on the main gate? Did you scale the wall?" He came close; he held her hand and said, "Maya! Maya! I did no such thing and I cannot even think of harming you. Please let me explain." "Look here Mister, you need a bloody good explanation for your crazy actions or I'll dial 100."

By now they had walked together to the bench kept nearby. He held her by her shoulders and made her sit on the bench; the can of pepper spray fell from her hand and rolled across the floor, away from them. His presence had had a strange effect on Maya.

The stranger sat next to her. She looked at him and said nervously, "Start talking." He looked at her with those deep-set eyes; Maya's heart skipped a beat. He asked, "What do you want to know?" Maya shook herself out of the stupor and said, "How about an introduction." "Yes, an introduction!!! Well, let's see. How do I introduce myself? You see, I don't get many chances to introduce myself." Maya gave him a look that could put a fire dragon's eyes to shame. He quickly started to talk, "You see I have always been with you and around you." Maya snapped at him, "What do you mean? Have you been stalking me? Are you a stalker? Now I get it." Maya started to get up. He pulled her down, made her sit again, and said, "That's your problem. You jump to quick conclusions. You draw assumptions and arrive at your own silly judgments. That is why you are so alone and lonely. You are so insecure that you doubt everyone and that has kept you friendless and single." Maya was spitting fire now, "Who are you to judge me and analyze my character and then rip it apart? How much do you know about me and my life?" He looked at her with kind of meditative eyes and asked, "Do you believe in God?" His look had a mesmerizing effect on her. She felt that she was kind of enjoying his company and felt a strong urge to open her heart to him. Even just arguing with him was kind of therapeutic. He had, it seemed cast a strange spell over her. So, as if in a trance she started to weave a reply, "How can I believe in something I have not seen?" He quickly said, "One doesn't need to see everything to believe, one can feel, one can experience." Maya contemplated, "Well if you ask me, if I feel His presence through my experiences then yes He is there somewhere. But then He is a horrible villain." He was again quick to answer, "Yes, I couldn't agree more but it only seems to us that way, He has a larger picture in front of him and thus his plans for us are also larger than we understand." Maya retorted, "What larger plan did He have for me by snatching both my parents away when I was just a baby? And now he has taken Granny away as well, rendering me alone and totally helpless in this whole wide world." The stranger smiled ever so slightly, holding her gaze he took a little longer to speak this time, "Well I cannot comment on that. It's not a part of my portfolio. There must have been worst pain waiting for them if they lived." Maya burst out laughing, "Bullshit! Who gives Him the right to decide whether any one of us, is capable of shouldering the pain or suffering that He Himself is inflicting upon us? First He writes our fate and then he makes us believe that whatever He chooses for us is for our good! And how silly we human beings are to believe in someone that we are not even sure exists? How do you know all this and do you want me to believe you? Who do you think you are? Are you some kind of a God-man? Hmmm? Or are you God Himself?" Nothing wiped out his smile, "I am not God but I am an Angel for sure. Look at me don't I look like one?" He got up and swiped his hand from his head to his toes and struck a pose like a model. Maya laughed again, "You are incorrigible. If you are an angel where are your wings?" "I don't have wings but I do have a shroud." He swirled on his toes and out of nowhere appeared a black shroud that he wore over his shoulders and when he faced her, she thought she would faint but he held her with utmost care and tenderness and held her by her shoulders. "Look at me." Maya had her eyes shut tight. He insisted, "Don't fear me. Yes, I am the Angel of Death. And your time has not come yet."

Maya opened her eyes ever so slowly. Yes, he looked like an angel of death. Yet he was handsome. She found her bearings and it took her a great effort not to let her voice shake, "If indeed you are The Angel of Death, what are you doing here? You should be in Ukraine, or in Israel, ruthlessly harvesting all the lives that have fallen there and are still falling? Not only the soldiers on both sides but innocent civilians, men women, and children alike." The stranger said, "I am there as well. You see I have to have the skill of being in multiple places simultaneously. My job is such. Nobody can escape my net if their time is up in this dimension." "Good for you. Glad that you dropped by. I wanted to meet you myself. In fact, I have been looking for you. You must be very happy to be able to net so many lives without much work." He, held her by her hand and invited her to dance with him, "Yes I am rejoicing. Come join me in my celebrations." Maya shrank and pulled her hand away. "If you indeed are the Angel of Death then you should be ashamed of yourself to come uninvited and pluck people away just like that. You must have held a feast during the pandemic. What do you do with all the lives you take away? Where do you put them? Does your heart not ache with the pain of those whose loved ones you take? You snatch away dear ones from dear ones without mercy. Do you have a heart or a mind for that matter? Does your conscience not poke you with guilt? Do you feel no shame in robbing people from people? Does your soul not cry when you orphan a child?" With every question Maya's anger rose by a notch and by the end, she was actually screaming. Exhausted she held her head between her two palms and sat down. The stranger…nay The Angel of Death said pensively, "I am the most hated one, I know but I am just doing my job. Like everyone else. Mind you, I do it well even if I am overworked. I do not complain. I am on call 24x7. No Sundays, and no holidays. Admire me for I have kept my schedule this way from time immemorial. If I take a break from my job Life would rot and decay. Then Life would chase me and you all would seek and beg me to continue with my job. So, think hard before you ask me all those accusing questions. If Death does not celebrate how will Life? Life is beautiful because Death exists. Life owes all her glory and beauty to the decay of Death. Then why dread me? Why fear me? I am the one who saves you in the end from all the hurts, all the pain, and all the misery that Life inflicts upon you. I am your saviour, your true friend. So, don't fear me. I only clean up the mess that Life creates and leaves behind." He sat down next to her.

Maya felt a sudden lightness in her head. She felt a strange glow that washed over her entire being and with that, she realized the truth of every word that this so-called Angel of Death had uttered. Yes, Death indeed is our ultimate soul mate, the friend that frees our souls from the prison of our bodies.

She looked at him and said, "There is truth in every word you said but what of the souls? Who saves our souls from all the hurt and all the pain? Where do you take them to heal?" He said looking right through her, "I am sorry, that, I cannot reveal." She pleaded but he didn't relent.

Helplessly she said, "I know you are just doing your job like everyone else but tell me why are you here today if it is not my time yet?" He looked deep into her eyes and said, "Sometimes, I need to appear by your side to remind you that I am right here, walking beside you all the time and you don't know when your time will come. So, make the best of the time that you still have in your account. Let me also tell you that you are the special one. I don't appear like this for everyone. My warnings are not so friendly. I might appear in the form of an illness, disease, accident, or grief. So, Maya, make full use of the time while Life offers it and I permit. Go out there, have fun, and live your life as you want. Everyone deserves that. Don't wait for the right time for there is no right time. Now is the time that is yours. Don't carry the burden of the departed. That was their fate. You have your own. Live your fate without any grief and guilt. Joy and gaiety are for you to snatch from life. Life only offers, it doesn't fill your platter. You have to make an effort and serve yourself. Don't waste your time in the grief that belongs to the past. What belongs to the past should be left in the past. Shed your grief and the shroud of guilt that you have worn all your life. You are not responsible for anything that you have not created. Yes, you are fully responsible for your own life. Don't pin the blame on others of the consequences of the choices that you make. When you make your own choices take full responsibility for the outcome of those choices." His smile turned into a broad grin as he stretched his hand once again, "Let's start from here. Join me, in celebrating your life. Come on Maya… the magically mystic with loads of courage……come on." He urged her. Maya took his hand this time without hesitation. She returned his smile as she joined him in his dance. She understood that life was a gift that needed to be cherished and that Death was not after all ugly.

The Angel of Death snapped his fingers and music came alive in surround system and they danced into the night. How long? Maya had no idea. But she knew her life had changed forever with that, one blind date.

* * * * * * *

Forever in Love

It was a gorgeous morning. The ocean breeze was fresh and invigorating. I sat comfortably on the deck chair of my beach home with my toes all toasty, tucked inside the soft shawl that I had draped around my shoulders, more for emotional soothing than any real cover from the chill. I held a large cup of green tea with both my hands wrapped around it for the same kind of comfort.

I have always been a morning person. There's a different almost magical quality to early mornings before the day kicks in and hits you with the very sobering normal, real, and routine. The birds were just stirring and the calm surf made it feel like even the ocean was just waking up and stretching. Being here felt meditative. It never failed to fill my soul and reset my mind. It was still twilight but in a minute or two the sun would show up to the party.

I let my gaze travel towards the distant horizon. But then it stopped. Halfway down the beach, I spotted a man and a woman walking hand in hand away from me, towards the ocean. Such a perfect handsome couple they made! They seemed to be made for each other. The sun peeped from behind my house so very stealthily, that I felt its arrival only when its soft rays danced in the woman's hair and created sparkling highlights. It was only then that I noticed that her hair was blondish brown. Her powder blue dress hugged her slim form and the hem flirted with her calves. His broad shoulders and easy gait made him look like the most handsome man I'd ever seen.

They walked slowly but their steps seemed sure and their faces were both turned up against the morning wind.

Hand in hand they kept walking away from me. And my eyes watched them lovingly. Suddenly I felt that the woman wavered, just a little, as if drunk on his love. The man reacted quickly and put his arm around her slender shoulder to hold her up. But the woman wavered some more. The man promptly swept her up in his arms the way one would carry a bride over the threshold into one's home for the first time. He held her and bent down. It looked like he kissed her on her forehead but they were now much further away so I couldn't see clearly. He didn't break his stride, even with her in his arms, he walked effortlessly towards the rolling surf.

The woman in blue looked at ease too, nestled in his arms, her hair blew with the breeze and her sheer dress fluttered around her dangling feet. He must have said something because she laughed and the sound carried over the waves.

Slowly he walked to the edge of the water with his eyes fixed it seemed on the face that was his love.... his life...his everything.

He kept walking. The water swum around his feet as the high tide came rushing in, then receded in an endless dance leaving shells and tiny crabs in its wake. But soon the water was up to his ankles. He kept walking and I watched them with affection and silently prayed for their love to keep growing till they got old together. The water had by now risen to his calves and soon his knees were submerged too. May they never be separated! That was the prayer on my lips.

I was so enthralled by the vision of this beautiful couple; I almost scalded my hand with the green tea. I patted the spill down and looked back, not wanting to miss a moment.

He was now hip-deep in the water. The woman's tumbling tresses were kissing the water. The sun was shimmering on everything now as if someone had just spilled a truckload of glitter. They made such a stunning picture together. I could not look away. But I felt a small tightness in my chest now.

He kept walking, wading against the advancing waves. Were they going for a swim fully clothed? This was not the best season for a swim. The water kept rising and my sense of strange unease got worse and worse.

The water was now around his waist and the woman in his arms was half in the water. I was in full panic by now. I was on my feet, waving my arms. My shawl fell to the floor as I yelled to warn them. Had they not seen the red flags on the beach? During these rainy months, the ocean was far too capricious and there were, '*No Swimming*' signs all over. But they seemed to be in a trance, blissfully unaware of the imminent danger.

I scrambled to find my phone and decided it would be faster if I got to them. I ran barefoot down the steps leading from the deck to the sands of the beach. My feet felt leaden and I was out of breath from shouting and running full speed but it felt like I was on a treadmill getting nowhere closer.

I started screaming wildly now but they didn't even notice me. Nor did anyone else because there was no one else around. Unusual, I remember thinking to myself but I had a more urgent crisis before me.

The woman in his arms had disappeared underwater! Oh my goodness, I was too late already! The man had water up to his shoulders now and he kept wading effortlessly and calmly, not once responding to my calls. And in no time he too went under.

They vanished as if dissolving in the massive ocean. They had just disappeared. No sign of them. As if they had never been there. I stood there the soft wet sand sinking below my feet, my hand at my gaping mouth. I couldn't move nor could I scream.

Holding my breath I just waited, suspended in time and perplexity. For a moment, I thought they were just fooling around and would emerge from the water, gasping for breath and laughing together like they had moments ago. Any minute...... I waited .....but nothing broke the surface of the sea. It was perfectly still. Even the wind and the surf seemed to have died. They were simply gone. No screams, no thrashing, no waves, as if they had just peacefully crossed over to another dimension.

I felt the water licking my toes and I tried to stumble back slowly towards the house. But it was like walking through a heavy bog. My legs felt heavy. I took a deep breath to fill my lungs but nothing came! I was choking. And there was no one to help. My palms were throbbing red hot. There was a searing pain in my chest. And sweat was now running in rivulets down my face, all the aquas of the sky and the sea got hazy and the horizon tilted as I buckled and my cheek hit the sand with a thud.

I woke with a start. My hand hit the bottle by my bedside. It crashed to the ground. The sound resounded in the quiet room. I was alone. The ceiling fan swam into view as I opened my eyes and tried to get my bearings.

I was not on the beach. I was in my own bed. I realized that I had been in a dream. Drenched in sweat, I took a full deep breath, grateful to feel the air rushing in. I kicked off the covers and just lay there, still numb and fuzzy from what I had experienced. I took some time to gather my thoughts and shake myself off. After all, it was only a dream. Your rational brain kicks in and analyzes it all but feelings have a way of lingering like wisps of smoke even hours afterwards. I felt sad and low. I tried to shake it off. I made a big cup of tea for myself and wrapped in my shawl, I walked out to my favourite morning nook on the deck. It was a beautiful morning. I took a few sips of my green tea and looked out onto the beach and the ocean beyond, half expecting to find the couple from my dream.

Instead, I saw a crowd gathered at the edge of the beach. My next-door neighbor came running towards my deck. He was sweaty and agitated as he spoke in short broken sentences while trying to catch his breath. "Can you believe it?... They found bodies! …A couple…pretty young. The cops don't know for sure. But they're saying it most likely happened very early this morning."

I froze as I listened intently and then asked in a quiet voice, "What were they wearing, Steve, do you know?"

He nodded, trying to catch his breath, and finally spoke, "That's what's odd. Not swimmers. She was in a blue dress and he was in a shirt sleeves. And they washed up on the sand in a tight embrace, like he was carrying her."

My heart started thumping so loudly it drowned out everything else he said after that. My knuckles got white and tight around my mug, the hot tea sloshed and scalded my hands, I shivered like an autumn leaf and the bile rose in my throat. Was this also a dream? It was unreal.

"I think I'm gonna be sick," I managed to murmur. My neighbor took the mug from me kindly and set it down. He draped the fallen shawl back on my shoulders and helped me sit back down in the chair.

I could not register a thing he was saying to me. It was too much to make sense of. I felt tired. And that sadness was back.

And dreams they say, never come true. But mine had! If I had somehow saved them in my dream could I have saved them in life? Could I have…?

* * * * * * *

The Stranger in My Room

Raghuvir Raghav was pacing in his room like a caged tiger. His thick tuft of unruly curls was even more disheveled than usual, hiding his thick glasses that were precariously propped up on his head. His long kurta and ankle-length pajamas fluttered with the small tides of air from his big strides as he walked up and down the room. The corner of his *pashmina* was holding onto his shoulder for dear life as most of it swept the floor behind him.

Shit, shit shit! I can't believe he's back! I don't know what he wants with me. He wrung his hands; there was dread in his eyes. He could feel his heart pounding like a wild animal. He was muttering and flailing his arms, trying to figure out his options. He just wanted to scream and shoo the intruder away. But he couldn't even dare to look at the corner where he was standing.

Raguvir knew, there was no avoiding this. He had to face him and just end this once and for all. He took a deep breath and tried to make his frightened, shaky voice as reasonable and calm as possible…'Look, I really don't know why you keep showing up here, uninvited. You stand here silently smiling like a goddamn psycho. I don't know what you want from me. I don't know you! Please leave me alone. I never forget a face. And I know this for sure, I have never seen you before.'

'What? Say something for God's sake! Are you here to kill me? You're driving me crazy, that's for sure. I've started seeing you in my dreams too now. It's terrifying! I'm afraid to go to sleep. Please, please I beg you. Kill me if that's what you're here to do. I don't care. Be done with it. At least this torture will end.' The stranger said nothing. He just stood there watching Raghuvir, a dark look in his eyes, as if secretly relishing the sight of this poor man unraveling before him like a tumbling ball of wool.

Spent from his outburst Raghuvir collapsed on the armchair. And for a few long minutes, the two of them just stared at each other. Each holding the other's gaze.

'Do you have any shame? Can you see how unreasonable you are being? You break in here. You don't tell me who sent you? What do you want? You stand there and just make me so furious!'

Nothing! No reaction.

He leapt up in anger, and the *Pashmina* gave up and fell to the floor, Raghuvir's voice reached a frenzied pitch, two impossible octaves higher, shrieking and crying, he reached for the glass by his bedside and threw it at the intruder. 'GET OUT GET OUT GET OUTTTTT!' The glass smashed into shards. He turned away and howled and wailed into the wall. After a few minutes, hoping that this had frightened the intruder off, he turned back.

'Unbelievable! Look at the man's nerve!' He was still there. 'What the hell!' Raghuvir clutched his curls in exasperation and started sobbing. His entire body shuddered as he crumpled on the carpet defeated, deflated. Simpering and negotiating now, 'Please, please, I have nothing to give you. You seem to be a decent chap, be kind and just leave, please. I really don't know you. You look at me like you know me. Do you? How? Stop smiling for God's sake and just say something! I swear to God, I'll kill you if you don't speak or get the hell out.'

Raghubir sighed wearily. He had no energy left now to even argue or explain. He felt like he had said all these exact same things earlier too. They never worked before so why would they now? He just wanted to be alone. Sit peacefully in solitude. Maybe he could lay down for a bit. 'So tired,' he muttered to himself. But how could he rest while that man just stood and watched him? He might be waiting just for that, for him to let his guard down so he could attack him. When he first moved here, Raghuvir had loved this place. He felt safe and at home here. The garden was pretty and he enjoyed the peace. His own personal space, no one to share it with or have inane conversations with! People were so lame. He was grateful for his sanctuary, no irritating visitors, no annoying 'friends' barging in. Until now!

The stranger was close enough to the door. Perhaps if he could take him by surprise, push him out, and quickly lock the door…

Chatter would distract him, thought Raghuvir so he bravely started inching forward as he talked, 'I have to give it to you, you are quite the trickster. I am amazed at how you keep sneaking in here day after day. I could have sworn I locked the door. Excellent skills! Did you ever work as a magician?' He smiled, amused by his own clever joke. Then he smirked and suddenly felt pity for this old man. Why had he been so afraid of him? Now that he looked closely at him, he realized he could easily overpower the fellow. He was slightly stooped and that sagging, sad, jowly chin, wrinkled hands, and crumpled *kurta*. He almost felt sorry for him.

'Are you lonely, old man? Is that why you keep wandering in here? I doubt we could be friends though. You look like you're close to the finish line. And me! I'm in my prime man. So many dreams, so much to accomplish, big ideas, bright future - the world is mine! You just wait and see. What would we even talk about? You with your regrets and so-called wisdom. Ha! I can see how well that worked for you.' He laughed again, mockingly this time. 'You think you can wear me down and get me to waste my time chatting and hanging out with you. No, thank you. Go find someone else. Get out! Get out! Get out!'

"What is the matter, Mr. Raghav? Why are you standing in the cold? Where is your shawl?" Asked Sameera, "Let me get it for you." She tried to enter the room. Raghuvir barred her entry blocking the open door with his arm. Putting a finger to his lips he whispered, "Be careful, don't enter the room he is there." Taking his cue, Sameera whispered back, "Who is there Mr. Raghav?"

"Remember, the man I told you about? He's back!" He hissed in anger – "I am so sick of him! I've tried everything but he's so infuriating! Do you know him? Can you help me get him out, please? I've threatened him, I've yelled at him, I don't know what he wants, I almost hit him but then I felt bad because he's so old. I think we should report him to the cops. I don't know. What do you think? My brain hurts. God! I just want this to end." Sameera listened kindly and said, "Yes, you are right, he can be frustrating;

let's see if we can get him out together, shall we?" She gently held him by his hand and guided him into the room. She picked up his shawl, wrapped it around his shoulders, and said softly, "Now Mr. Raghav show me where is he?" With bewildered eyes he looked at her and wagged his finger desperately, "Sister Sameera! What's wrong with you? Can't you see him standing there? He is right there."

Sameera smiled and said, "Yes, yes of course I can see him. He is right there. You don't worry; I know how to get him out of here. He will never ever bother you again. Why don't you sit down for a second, I will go get help."

Annoyed, she went out into the corridor to look for the warden...

"I don't care if he's a new ward boy, you should have briefed him about this when he started. Why did he have to uncover the mirror in Mr. Raghav's room? He was doing so well and now…" she shook her head in frustration. Send two ward boys with me and just move that mirror out of the room, right now please."

* * * * * * *

Trapped

Oh! How happy she was to be free, to go wherever she wanted, whenever she fancied! Playfully rumbling and tumbling, up and down, over the mountainsides. Clean and crystal clear in every eddy, in every wave, a pure soul, that is who she was. Her days were spent, shimmering and reflecting the sunshine back into the universe and at night she was a dancing floor for the moon.

Nothing could stop her from flowing; no rocks, no pebbles, no twists, no turns, no sudden falls. She could handle anything that life threw her way, endlessly flowing with grace no matter what unfolded before her. Fearlessly carving her way around big boulders and through thick forests, she danced with joy. How alive and unstoppable she felt! Free to flow wherever nature took her, from icy banks and vast snowfields to spring greens and summer blooms. Splashing life along the way, painting her banks with colours of joy; grassy greens and buttercup yellows there, roughly kissed lips of rambling red roses here, drops of violet irises and blue forget-me-nots…all this beauty burst into life where there were just muddy browns before.

Her journey never felt dull. So much to see, so many places to be. She lived in the moment, never worrying about the next. No time to waste on remorse or sorrow. She was filled to the brim with happiness and made others around her just that...happy! Undaunted by fate and unafraid of the future, she had thought, like most of us do that her life would go on like this forever and ever. But nothing lasts forever, does it? No circumstance, no relationship, no love, no hate, no friendship, no animosity...nothing...absolutely nothing is forever.

And so her joy too was not destined to last.

One day, the cosmic womb rumbled deep within, a low ominous growl. Far away at first but then louder, bigger, stronger. The magnificent peaks shuddered in the skies, and the very earth upon which they stood started slipping and falling away. The mountains started to tumble and collapse upon themselves, sending flying crashing demons of rock and debris in every direction. The sound was deafening. The air was now so thick with dust, that you could barely see the great big boulders and the storm of stones whirling and kicking and shooting like thousands of manic, possessed dervishes. Giant trees got uprooted and flung like mere twigs. One crashed right into her; crushing her and blocking all exits. Everywhere she looked there were rocks and earth and roots and havoc. Could she turn back perhaps? No! No way out. A massive range of cliffs had fallen behind her and blocked the mouth of her origin. Furiously trying to work out her options and frantically looking for a path, even just a small one, she kept telling herself to stay calm. But there was no way forward. Even if she somehow managed to go around the colossal trunk and the boulders, there was another imploded mountain in front. She stopped. What was the point?

Hope started fading as rapidly as the daylight. Darkness set in; in the skies and deep in her heart. The fear of stagnation crept in slowly from the edges. It moved in, inch by inch towards the core of her being. She rose up in anger. Thrashing, heaving, pushing, smashing furiously but nothing budged. She summoned all her strength and whipped herself into a huge tsunami that came crashing down but the mountains had moved enough. They stood still now.

She was trapped for good.

Grief hit her like a slap in the face. Steep mountains had surrounded her from all sides. Gloom set in and deep, deep depression seized her from within. Black inky night fell heavy around her. All her energy suddenly evaporated. It felt like the life was draining out of her. Her once clear pure soul started to become murky, stale, and toxic. She stood there in utter bewilderment not knowing what to do.

How to be? Who to be? She had never known life the way it stood today. She felt so tired. So tired. She just wanted to curl up and die.

Morning came and the sun glinted across her again. She stood perfectly still, for the first time ever. She looked around. Taking it all in. She never had before been still. The morning sun twinkled on her ripples ethereally, a sharp contrast against the wrecked surroundings.

She tried to assess the damage. Without the turbulent emotions of the night, she saw what her situation was, a little more objectively. It was far from good. There was no escaping reality. The hard truth was that her entire life had changed. Her circumstances had dramatically altered forever. She would never be the same river again. Her character, her personality, her nature… it all would alter too. She didn't even feel like herself.

There were no choices left; she was trapped in time and space. She could see, hard as it was to face it, that it was impossible for her to break free again. She felt helpless and her helplessness turned into restlessness and restlessness into anger and anger into boundless rage. This cycle of emotions went on for weeks. She would start thrashing against the mountains that had entrapped her but they were too mighty, unmoving, and strong for her. They were not imaginary they were very real and very formidable and intimidating. There was no way she was going to be able to escape from this prison. How she longed to flow wild and free like she used to. Oh, how she would give anything to be free once more but there was no way she could buy her freedom. There were no bribes, no negotiations no bargains…none.

Eventually, a strange calm came over her. All her anger spent crashing against the steep cliff faces, she became pensive.

She tried to quiet her restless soul like a mother soothing a tantrum-throwing toddler. It started to work. The realization came slowly and painfully but with startling clarity…like when muddy water settles and you can see the truth reflected on the clear surface. The only way out of this situation was, acceptance.

She had never known serenity. She kind of liked it. What does one do? Give up, being? No. The answer was a big NO. She had to face the situation she found herself in and try to make the best of it. Suddenly an insight emerged from deep within. She had to be who she had become now and stop yearning for who she used to be or who she could have been. She had to find the best path forward while staying still. There were many possible upsides to this new changed reality. How could she focus her attention on all that and not the past?

It dawned on her suddenly- She was a carefree, spirited mountain stream always on the move but now she was this peaceful, magnificent lake.

She closed her eyes and peered within– it was deep and still, placid and silent. Exquisite in its own way! All kinds of different life and colours were starting to stir and be born into existence. Including some freshwater springs that were beginning to burst forth!

The sun still shone on her waters, the moon still visited her every night. She was once again filled with joy and felt this strong desire to enjoy being what she was.

Once she realized this, she put all her energy into becoming the world's most beautiful freshwater lake teeming with life blood. Still, but never stagnant.

* * * * * * *

My Sister's Cottage

What an intense, hectic week it had been. I couldn't wait to get away for the weekend. We, my sister, and I have these cottages out in the Sahyadris. We found these adjacent plots and built ourselves these hide outs a few years ago when not many people were buying land here in these parts of the Western Ghats. The two properties, my sister's and mine are separated only by a picket fence. Though we have separate main gates, we are internally connected through a small gate in the picket fence. All the cottages and grounds are carved out of a mountainside. My cottage is right at the top and my sister's is on the third terrace.

What I love most about this place is that it's just about a two-hour drive from the airport and on a good traffic day, barely an hour away from our apartment in town. You can't ask for an easier weekend getaway. In just 60 minutes you can go from the frenzy of zig-zagging two-wheelers and ever-growing traffic in ever ever-expanding city of Pune to the most tranquil terraced gardens. It is quite literally like sitting in the lap of nature - green rolling forests, crisp fresh air, birdcalls, and almost no annoying neighbours. While the sunsets are pretty special there, it is the sunrises that take your breath away. One of the many reasons, I love the early mornings.

My wife, Kalpana, and I drove up on Friday night, looking forward to some time alone away from the loving but rather large family we have.

Since we have our own key to the cottage and had packed our dinner we did not disturb the caretakers. They had long retired to their own quarters. Ganesh and his wife are well accustomed to this routine. I opened a can of beer and poured my wife a glass of her favourite Nasik Red. Taking off the weight of the week like a heavy backpack, I cracked my back and we both flopped gratefully into the rather worn-out chairs on the veranda. The night sky was a clear deep blue and pierced with stars. Back in Pune, I hardly ever saw any. Some stray soft clouds were flirting with the full moon. Countless fireflies were twinkling throughout the expanse of both the gardens spread out below us and the forest in the surrounding hills. It felt like the sky and the earth had become one. Was that a star or a light in a village? Below in the valley, some loner was playing on an *ektara*. What a perfect evening, just what I needed. In about twenty minutes Kalpna went in for a refill and came back out. Mellow and quiet as well. She stood against the railing and looked beyond into the valley. She could see my sister's cottage. The dim night light was on. She loved the French glass windows in my sister's cottage. She took a slow sip and stood there admiring them.

I knew she wanted us to get large bay windows at our cottage too. So I was half expecting her to bring it up again but instead, she said, "Ajay, am I drunk already or am I seeing things?" I got up from my chair and lovingly put my arm around her shoulder and said, "No darling you never get drunk! Why do you ask?" She pointed to my sister's cottage and said hesitantly, "See, the swing in Deedi's living room is swinging. Isn't it?" I followed her gaze through the foliage; yes indeed I could see the large swing through the foliage swaying gently.

"Oh! That? Ganesh's little rascals must have been playing in there, I'll have a word with him tomorrow," I said. "Kids will be kids after all." I had a nice buzz by now. And I knew my wife too well after all these years, jumpy by nature, everything was something with her, so I started using my calm voice and it worked...and thankfully we started to chat about the caretaker and his most recent foibles and the swing was forgotten.

We enjoyed the rest of the evening and the simple but sumptuous dinner that we had carried with us.

Around midnight we retired to our favourite bedroom that was upstairs. This room had large windows that opened to the valley view and also to my sister's cottage.

The view from here was the best on the entire property.

I opened the window and drank in the sights before turning in. The dark mountains and the blanket of stars met my eyes. My soul always felt like a dusty mirror wiped clean whenever I came here. As I gazed out into the night sky, I saw something moving from the corner of my eye. It was the swing visible through the window at my sister's cottage. It was still swaying with the same gentle rhythm. I rubbed my eyes and looked again. Yup, there it was, through the gap in the foliage down below, clearly still swinging. My buzz was suddenly gone and my mind kicked into full gear. So strange! There's got to be an explanation. The kids can't be in there so late. Was it the drinks that for some reason had not sat well with us today? Could it just be the fog and the dim light playing tricks? I did not want to worry Kalpna. I shook my head and said to myself, 'Whatever it is we shall deal with it in the morning. Maybe the kids were fooling around. But then why couldn't I see them?' With all these unsettled thoughts still swirling in my head, I climbed under the covers. It wasn't long before the busy day and the drive caught up with me and I was out like a bad opening batsman.

Did I tell you about the sunrises here? Yes, I think I did. Spectacular! I'm an early riser anyway but when I'm here I make sure I never miss them. I woke up just after 5.30 the next morning. It was still dark outside but I was wide awake, force of habit. I had forgotten about the swing in my sister's cottage. I got out of my bed and shuffled over to the window, deciding whether I should go for a walk or just sit with my tea on the patio. Suddenly my gaze went to my sister's cottage and it all came back, the weird swing thing from the previous night.

You won't believe it but to my horror, the swing was still moving. I felt a chill go down my spine. Now in the cold hard well, not light of day yet but you know what I mean, it was not so easy to write it off. I was sober and well rested, there was no fog and the swing really was moving. As if someone was sitting on it but not visible. Who is in there and why? I was sure that someone from the caretaker's family had decided to sleep in the cottage which they were not supposed to do. I got angry at the thought. But I also knew that the caretakers were a good honest lot. They had been with us for many years. Had someone broken in? Squatters? It was unheard of, in these parts though. But the swing looked so odd, the way it was swaying...almost like a... The hills around here were rife with stories about ghosts and spirits. Even the caretakers would talk about their encounters. It's the thick jungles, the wilderness, and the dark winding roads, people feel vulnerable and start seeing things. All the villages in the valley had their own local resident ghost if you please. I used to find it hilarious, all this illiterate, superstitious nonsense. The Goat stealing Ghost and the Banyan tree Ghoul…didn't seem that funny or far-fetched now as I watched that damn swing in the window.

Either way, I was determined to find out before daybreak.

I left my wife sleeping, picked up my flashlight, and went downstairs. From the verandah, I picked up one of the thick strong bamboo sticks that we keep there to scare off the monkeys and other wild animals that drop in uninvited from time to time. I started to walk down to my sister's cottage. I had no idea who or what I was going to meet there. Halfway down the sloping garden, I got a clearer view of the sitting lounge through the large kitchen window. I stood there transfixed. My throat suddenly felt dry and the stick in my hand didn't seem like it could offer any protection. The sitting room was absolutely empty. It was a studio layout so I could see straight through from where I was standing; there was no one in the kitchen and the bedroom area either. Not a soul.

The swing continued to move eerily back and forth at the same lazy pace. I could not believe my eyes.

I'm an engineer and science is my religion. I am the annoying person at dinner parties interrogating the supernatural and debunking mystical gossip. But this morning I didn't feel so sure of myself and what I believed to be true. Feeling like a little boy who's afraid to look under his bed, I had to keep talking to myself to keep walking. 'There's nothing to be afraid of. You're being irrational now. Keep going and you'll see, there will be a perfectly reasonable explanation. Just a couple more steps, come on, you can do it!' I made loud noises with the stick, cold sweat trickling down the small of my back, my eyes peeled on the swaying swing, one more step and then another.

Maybe I was wrong. Just because we have no proof yet, doesn't mean ghosts don't exist, my pragmatic brain was packing up. I heard myself muttering the *Hanuman Chalisa* under my breath. Even I was surprised. How did I remember it? Fear can make you do the strangest things I suppose.

It was too late to turn back and get help. I was now on the verandah; close enough to hear the muffled creaking of the hook from which the swing was suspended. And was that a soft groan of the wood, as if someone shifting their weight on it?! I watched in horror, my eyes stinging from not blinking.

The *Hanuman Chalisa* came out faster and faster in a desperate hiss, but I could only hear my own deafening heartbeat! Oh dear God, was that a little depression on the cushion? What the hell!? Maybe I should run, yes, run back. Oh shit, I can't breathe... I'm gonna die...I squeezed my eyes shut. Shouldn't have. Because I felt someone's breath, right on my neck and then something touched my shoulder- a blood-curdling scream came out of me. My terror echoed in the wilderness, waking up every bird, insect and villager in the valley.

"*Gud marning Sahbji*...? Sorry, I didn't mean to startle you." It was Ganesh the caretaker. I took a huge deep breath, the blood came flooding back to my extremities and I opened my eyes to look up, above the swing. The fan! The ceiling fan was moving gently. What a fool I had been. Hahahaha! Relief washed over me. I felt like a total idiot. All this cursed overactive imagination. I cleared my throat and turned around to face Ganesh with whatever little dignity I could muster.

"*Han! Han!* Good Morning, good morning Ganesh. How are you?" Anger is the easiest refuge of fools, isn't it? It was time for poor Ganesh to feel the full force of mine. "*Arey*, what is happening here? Where have you been all this time? And how many times have I told you to double-check everything before you sleep? Why did you leave the fan on in the cottage? Do you know what the electricity bills are like these days? I'm warning you, I will cut it from your salary if this keeps happening!" Oh thank God, I was feeling foolish but relieved. I could picture how hard Kalpana would laugh at me when I told her everything.

Poor old Ganesh stood there in the ethereal glow of the morning sun that had just started to emerge from behind the mountains. He apologized profusely. His hands together pleading forgiveness, bending lower and lower as he spoke – "Sorry Sahbji, I am so sorry, I …uhm…checked all the switches and I locked all the windows last night." His hand nervously went to his pocket from where he produced the key and started fumbling with the main door. "…I'll just check, I thought I had…but I'm extremely sorry if I forgot to…Sahbji, where, I mean, which fan is on?"

I turned back towards the window with a righteously indignant face and an accusatory finger wagging hard, "Look, that one!"

The swing was still. And so was the fan. Deathly still! My finger still suspended in the air, I turned back to look at Ganesh and then back at the swing. Nothing! As the bright morning sun flooded the cottage interior, it all looked so solid and real and normal and everything I had seen, felt and heard, seemed unreal and ridiculous. But I knew what I had seen.

Or did I? Wait a minute. Was there a depression in the cushion on the swing that was still now? Or was I imagining? Was there in fact a Ghost swinging away the whole night in my sister's cottage that had come only to meet me? I am still wondering.

* * * * * * *

Causeway

I woke up with a pleasant feeling.......felt no pain in my brain and no ache in my heart.......as if intoxicated. At last, he had come for me. He stood by my bedside. I looked up at him, with accusing eyes. He just smiled back at me. That smile of his as always, melted my heart and all my anger vanished. He offered his hand and I held it with full faith and trust. I had complete belief that he had come for me and would take me along, wherever he had been, all this while.

He held my hand and I rose from my bed. He led me and I followed as we both started to walk.

My feet were light, my heart was soaring and I walked with him hand in hand in a trance. We walked through the house, out through the door and out into the garden. We kept walking down the garden path that was so familiar and strewn with white blossoms, again familiar. We walked carefully as not to trample over the fallen flowers.

We walked in silence as we had done so often in the past. We rarely needed words to converse. Just being together, walking hand in hand was blissful… always. I felt so light in my body and mind that I was sure I could fly, if I tried.

Thus we walked without any hurry as if neither of us wanted to reach our destination. We walked through the garden gates, into the woods and then through the woods down to the mountain stream where we sat on a rock, dangling our feet over its edge till the gurgling cold water tickled our toes. The soft morning sun rays were dancing on the water and we watched in silence, soaking in the beauty of nature and the joy of being together once again. The feeling was simply blissful.

He put his arm around my shoulder and held me firmly.

I had so many questions for him. Why had he left? Why so suddenly? Why without a goodbye? Why had he left without leaving a kiss on my lips? Why? Why for God's sake had he taken a decade to return? Why? Why? There were so many questions he needed to answer. He looked at me and I knew that he could read the questions in my eyes. He didn't say a word, he just smiled and held my gaze.

Suddenly, I needed no answers. The fact that he was back, was enough for me. I didn't care for anything else, anymore. Once again, I felt complete. What could be better than he being by my side with his arm around my shoulder! Nothing in the world meant anything to me than this moment. I had waited a full decade for this moment; I was not going to lose it to any explanations. I just didn't need any, now that he was here.

The air was heavy with the fragrance of the spring blooms. I wanted to hold that moment forever but deep in my heart, I knew the spell would break. Though he did not speak, my thoughts were his too. I could see it in his eyes, the thought that crossed his mind, 'You still can read my mind!' I smiled back in affirmation.

He held my hand tighter, turned my face towards him and gently planted a kiss on my forehead and then he rose.

I panicked, 'No, you are not leaving. Not again.' I wanted to say. No, I wanted to yell but could not find my voice.

A deep chill filled my heart but a sliver of hope rose somewhere in that dark chill, 'May be he has come to take me with him.' He started to walk; I held his hand and walked with him. We were now standing in a strange forest by a riverside. The water was blue, peaceful and calm. It seemed as though it was not moving yet, I knew, it was flowing. The forest ran along the river banks. Morning mist rose from the water surface and moved lazily skyward. Gradually the mist thickened and weaved its way through the trees engulfing the forest ever so slowly but surely. I was certain that the forest on the other bank would soon vanish. He left my hand and started walking down the bank towards the water.

I started to follow him. He asked me to stop with a movement of his hand. My feet froze midway and I stopped there, unable to move. He had cast some kind of a spell on me with that slight movement of his hand. I was rooted.

I wanted to tell him, 'I am no longer scared of water. I have overcome my hydrophobia. I can even swim now, please take me along,' but I could neither move nor could I find my voice or words. It seemed as if I was frozen and imprisoned in my own aura.

I could now see him wading through the peaceful water. No, wait a minute. It seemed that he was gliding over the water surface. How could it be? Where had he learnt this? Or am I going crazy? As I said, I was rooted to the ground, unable to move as if my body had turned into stone. He went on without looking back, wading through the water or sailing over it, I could not tell. He was on the other bank, now. He turned to look at me and smiled. The smile on his face was shadowed by a heavy gloom and sadness crept in those intense eyes. My heart bled.

I suddenly heard him whisper in my ears as if he was standing right behind me but I could see that he was standing across the river, wrapped in the thin mist. What games was my mind playing with me? He whispered, 'Darling, I can't take you with me yet. You know, don't you? The orders come from above. Orders have not come yet. Someday, I will come for you but today is not the day. I do not have the orders yet.'

'Damn the orders.' I wanted to yell but I could not. I wanted to curse the authorities and the systems that sucked but I could not utter a word.

Then I saw him wave a goodbye. Pain had wiped off the smile from his face. He turned his back towards me and started to walk away, through the misty woods till everything got lost in a thick blanket of fog and I could see him no more.

I was drenched in gloom. The pain in my brain returned with full intensity and my heart ached as if some cold iron hand had gripped it in its strong fist. My knees melted and I sank to the ground, heavy under the burden of grief yet, not able to scream. I just sat there like a helpless wreck. I don't remember for how long.

I could not believe that he came after a decade and just left without any explanation or justification for his absence. I was drenched in misery. My numb mind was wrestling to find answers to so many questions and it left me drowned in an ocean of eternal hopelessness.

Does he want me to just wait for him another decade by this riverside? This question popped in my head and with that thought, a sudden surge of anger rose within me, pumping whole lot of energy into me. Angry energy oozed from every cell of my body. This was not fair, not fair at all. There was immense anger but not enough to wash my grief away. Somewhere deep in my heart, I knew that it was not his fault. He too did not want to leave but he seemed to be governed by some unknown force. I got up and with a heavy heart started to walk back to the house. Alone! There was no spring in my step and no joy in my heart. My feet were heavy; each step was an effort but I had to keep walking. So I kept walking back, alone, hoping with every step that he would appear quietly, hold my hand and walk me home.

No such thing happened. I dragged myself to my door step and rang the bell. No one opened the door for me because there was no one to open the door. There was no one waiting for me at home. There must be someone. I rang the bell again.

The doorbell rang, loud and shrill. I was in my bed. My feet found my slippers and my body waded through the house while my being was still in that mystic place. I opened the door for my house keeper and waded back to my room. I looked at my watch and the date hit me ....14th of July.....exactly a decade back on this date my soul mate had left me and crossed over leaving me behind.

Madhuri, my house keeper following me asked, "Deedi, have you been out in the garden in your house shoes?" I looked down at my feet and to my surprise my house slippers were indeed drenched in mud and dry leaves from the garden.

That is when I wondered, had I been in a dream? If yes, then what can explain my soiled slippers? Or is there actually a 'Causeway' between the two worlds ...here and beyond... like the No Man's Land between two countries.... where we could meet from time to time? Had I just returned from there?

****

Whispers in the Attic

They had slept in separate rooms again. The poor dog torn by the hard choices - whose feet to curl up at? Whose side to take? Who to comfort? Their fights were getting increasingly frequent. The same old grooves, the same patterns. Like a deja-hate-you. She was so spent, crying and arguing over the same stuff, over and over again. Maybe Nikhil and her had been together too long. They both knew exactly where to hurt each other… all the secret places where the old wounds were.

She couldn't even remember how it started this time but she was just grateful to be out of the house this morning. 'Grateful', jeez, that sounded horrible because poor old Suprabha Aunty was very sick. Ria leaned her head against the car window and closed her cried out eyes as they went round the hair pin bends. Guilt rose up like bile. She should have come up to visit her more. After Ria's parents died, Suprabha Aunty was the only family she had left. She had immediately gathered up little Ria and brought her to her ancestral home in the hills outside Ranikhet. It was always filled with love and clouds.

She had vivid, colourful memories of the place. All those different fruit trees and flowers she had never seen in the plains and the caretaker's daughter Gauri, a k a her partner in crime, laughing and whooping on that big old swing. Ria sighed heavily. She hadn't seen Gauri in years either. But you know how it is. Life gets in the way. Work, Nikhil, friends, deadlines, dinners, meetings…always something more urgent, greedily stealing your time and attention. It takes sickness or death to make you finally jump in a car and make the time for stuff that matters. She shook her head and wished she had visited more…

It was dusk by the time Ria's car pulled up at the gates of Cloud Cottage. A bizarrely modest name for the sprawling bungalow with its huge orchards and terraced gardens.

She saw some cars parked in the driveway. May be she was too late. A wave of sadness and even more stinging guilt gripped her.

She walked hesitantly towards the house, steeling herself for impact.

She knew even before she pushed the door open. All the furniture had been pushed back against the walls and clean white sheets were covering the rich Kashmiri carpets in the large sitting room. Her heart sank; she was late. Way too late.

Suprabha Aunty lay in the center of the room, dignified even in death. She was dressed in one of her famous Thanjavur silk saris. Her favourite gold and emerald ring glistened on her lifeless finger. She looked peaceful and graceful in death as she had in life.

Gauri had called Ria the previous day saying that Suprabha Aunty had suddenly become very unwell and was asking for her every time she came to, from her reoccurring bouts of unconsciousness. So here she was but alas dear old Suprabha Aunty was not. She had passed away a few hours back.

Gauri saw Ria enter the room and came running to her. She took her into her arms and burst out crying. Ria threw her arms around her and held her tightly. Tears rolled down their cheeks. They stood there for a long while. Crying for Suprabha Aunty and for all the missed ocean of time that stood between them that was now impossible to wade back through.

The room was packed with people from the neighbourhood who had known and loved Suprabha Aunty for many years.

But there was no family except for Ria. No one knew why Suprabha Aunty had never married. Ria had asked her mother but could never get her to talk about it, till one day she cornered Suprabha Aunty and asked her. She had just laughed and said, 'Never met anyone I could think of sharing my entire life with. And guess what? Who would look after Papaji's property and bake you such scrumptious cakes! Hnmm?' That was the end of that. Suddenly her mouth was filled with the delicious memory of her peach cake and fresh tears rolled down her cheeks.

Darkness fell sooner in these parts, and when it came it was pitch black. In a matter of minutes the looming ranges were like giant lumps of coal. It was decided that the cremation would take place the following morning.

Lots of people volunteered to stay the night.

It was late by the time everyone had found a place to retire. Ria lowered the volume of the bhajans that had been playing in the background. She sat next to her aunt, her gaze fixed on her face. It looked angelic in the dim light of the earthen lamp that was kept near her head. She whispered a sorry and without any warning more tears came.

Gauri softly padded over and said, "You must be tired after your long drive Ria. We have a long day ahead of us, why don't you go and get some rest?" Ria didn't want to leave, how could she leave Suprabha Aunty lying here? But Gauri gently pulled her up. "We'll be right here with her. Don't worry. It's the same room, the one you love. She made us keep that room always ready for you but you never …" Ria took a sharp breath in and her face contorted in agony. Gauri, whispered, "Sorry, I didn't mean to hurt you." Ria shook her head and they hugged good night.

Oh how she loved this little blue room next to the library in the attic. It had been her favourite hideout ever since she first came to this house. She would stare for hours at the blue latticework on the windows. She could easily slip into the library where her Nanu, when he was alive, would be sitting at his desk working on the accounts of the estate. She would spend hours reading.

She flopped down on the bed and tried to sleep. Her eyes stung when she closed them. The fight with Nikhil and now Suprabha Aunty just gone, the whispering people in the hall, the unsettling quiet in the valley…it all just got twisted and jumbled up inside. Her heart ached, her head throbbed, no tears came. She lay there in a haze, shoes still on, too tired to move, too tired to sleep.

That's when she heard it. It sounded like a whisper. Was it a dream? She rubbed her bleary eyes and tried to listen carefully. There! Again! Some whispers. Suddenly she was wide-awake. There was no one in her room. But it had sounded like it was right here. Maybe it was some of the neighbours outside.

She started to drift off. But then she heard it again. Someone was calling out. It was a whisper but it was urgent. She sat upright and held her breath. It was coming from the library. Or was it from the window? Now hyper alert, all the fatigue suddenly vanished, she prowled around listening, a little scared but mostly intrigued.

She cracked the door open and heard it again - the sound of muffled whispers, like someone whimpering in some kind of pain. How odd! Even in the cool mountain air, she could feel herself sweating now. And her heart pounded loudly. Too loudly. Shhhhh!

She stepped out into the dimly lit corridor. The old planks creaked underfoot. She had been right. It was the library. She turned the knob, threw the door wide open and flicked the switch. The whimpering stopped. There was no one here. Not a soul. She thought she was going insane. May be it was just her weary mind playing tricks on her.

She knew that she was the only one there so she wasn't sure why but she called out, "Who is there? Come out now!" Again she looked around just to make sure that no one was there. Nothing. She started to move to the door when suddenly someone whispered, 'Don't go, please don't go.' Then there was silence. "Who is there? Show yourself and I will not go." Said Ria who was beyond baffled now.

'Turn around and walk to the shelf that is right behind you. Yes, come on. Come closer.' Ria was so perplexed. What the hell was going on? Was this whole thing just a bad dream? Stories of spirits and ghosts up here in the mountains were not uncommon especially when someone passed on. But Ria was a rationalist. She shook herself awake and forced herself to walk to the book shelf as directed. Perhaps there was a hidden chamber behind this book shelf like in the movies.

She started to run her fingers over the spines of the books stacked there to check if there was a catch or a lever and the shelf would move to reveal a hidden chamber; and a perfectly reasonable explanation for all these strange whisperings. As her finger travelled from spine to spine, the voice hissed, 'Yes, stop there,' she checked out the book. It was 'The Golden Treasury' she stopped. This was a collection of poems, she knew. She had seen it in Suprabha Aunty's hands many times. 'Pull it out.' Came the whisper and she obeyed. 'Flip through it,' came the request. She did exactly what she had been asked to do. As she flipped through the pages something flew out of the book and fell to the floor. She bent down and saw an old large dry rose just next to an old faded picture of a handsome young man in uniform. She picked up the picture and turned it over. In faded ink she read the words written there, 'For you my dearest Suprapha, till I come back,' it was signed Amardeep and dated some 55 years back.

'Pick me up also.' Ria jumped, startled, she looked down on the floor at the rose in bewilderment. 'Have I gone crazy? Is that dry rose talking to me?' 'Yes, it is, I mean I am, I have been trying to call you. Thank God you found me. You can take me to her. I want to join her on the funeral pyre.'

Ria picked up the rose carefully from the floor and placed it on her palm and asked, 'What do you mean. People dry flowers all the time in their books.'

'Sure they do, but I am special. It was all very long ago but I remember it well. You see that young man in the picture? He was madly in love with Suprabha. Judging from how many times she caressed me and read these poems and wept quietly looking at his photo, she loved him too if you know what I mean. I, young lady, have had the privilege of being the very first and the only flower that he gave her along with his picture before he left.'

'She kept me along with his picture in her favourite book where we waited and waited and longed and pined but he was never to return. I stayed here for all these decades. She used to come up from time to time, be with us and we would read and sit and remember but it just made her sad so she came up less and less and lately she could not climb the stairs so these poems and I just sat here lonely, waiting and hoping. Today I heard she too has left forever.'

'True love is so rare, blessed are the ones who get to taste it even if it is only for a few days. If you find a real connection in this lifetime, make sure you treasure it. Sorry if I sound like a poem, it's the company I've been keeping all these years. Ha! Now please take me to her won't you? What better way to go than to go along with the love for which I was plucked from the garden?'

Ria was speechless. She had so many questions. But they all just faded. She was overwhelmed and felt so much love and loss as she pictured her young Aunt reading by the window looking out and waiting day after day, year after year…she suddenly came to. The incessant ringing of her phone pierced her reverie. It was Nikhil. He sounded so worried because she hadn't texted to tell him she'd reached safely. Her face softened. She smiled and said, I'm fine, I promise, don't worry, I'm sorry…they talked way into the night like the old days.

In the morning she woke up early and went downstairs where the preparations for the funeral had begun. She quietly went to where Suprabha Aunty lay and hid the faded picture and the dry rose in the folds of her sari. Did Ria see a smile playing on Suprabha Aunty's lips or was it just her imagination?

* * * * * * *

The Fifth Season

I stand in this solitary wilderness by myself, lonely, discarded, and disowned. No one has come to visit me in over a decade. Seasons have come and gone, time marches on, yet I stand still. I have watched the beauty of countless springs and summers, the calm of winter snow, the fresh greens of spring, and the riot of summer blooms. A feast for anyone's eyes but wasted on me. My soul aches with a sadness that no words can describe…what good is all the joy in the world if you have no one to share it with? All this beauty, to drink in, but like a miserable friendless drunk, no one to raise a glass with.

All by myself, I watched as the blossoms turned into fruits that no one plucked, no one tasted. The bounty of nature, wasted on the world. Ripe and rotten, they smashed to the ground.

The fiery colours of autumn came and went. No one marveled at all this great beauty. I tried to pass the time by counting all the shades of red. But year after year, it was the same. I felt especially desolate and forlorn when the winter came.

Biting winds came from the North, howling all around me. I shivered and shuddered and longed for someone to light a fire or give me a warm hug. But I stood alone, feeling sorry for myself, braving the onslaught of the snow flurries and the icy gales. Driven pure snow everywhere, as far as the eye could see. But nobody walked on it man or animal. Not a single footprint. No sign of life. And then it melted into a filthy slush all around me. Rinse and repeat. This went on year after year till I lost count, till I lost all sense of time and meaning. Why was I cursed? Why was I still here? Did nothing matter anymore?

I don't even complain these days. What's the point? No one is listening. There is, only *me,* standing here endlessly, patient on good days and just ready to give up and collapse on most other days. From sunrise to sunset, in complete silence, I keep waiting! Waiting for the fifth season!

If no one is listening, then why do I go on talking? Because I must tell my story...before it is too late... I must talk to someone, perhaps to time itself. It is like a silent spectator, a witness to it all, and who knows? One day time might tell my story to the times that are yet to come for only time knows that once upon a time I did not stand alone in this wilderness.

There was life teeming all around me. Children squealing and running around, grandfather smoking hookah, hacking coughs notwithstanding, dinners cooking, enticing smells wafting from room to room, fresh laundry billowing on the line, crying babies, yelling mothers, passionate debates, quiet conversations, music, laughter, busy bustling mornings, cozy, lazy evenings with everyone snuggled around a fire, sharing blankets, tired kids finally falling asleep in warm laps to softly whispered lullabies… so much, rich, glorious life abounded all around me.

And, my favourite, little Heer always so sweet and gentle. Like a dainty little fairy floating in and out. Her two brothers, one younger and one older, loved her so dearly. I saw them growing up together. I still remember the day; she was born…her impossibly tiny pink wrinkled fingers… She grew up to be such a beautiful young woman. A face like a full moon with stars sparkling in her eyes. Altaf and Asif grew up tall and strapping. And a few seasons later, they found a nice girl for Altaf.

That night, how I wished I could dance and join in! The air was alive with revelry. I had never hosted such a big celebration before. The smells and sounds and sights of the engagement mixed with the scent of night Jasmines at the open windows. New clothes for everyone, teetering stacks of boxes of *mithai,* jewelry, and *pashminas* and so much laughter and noise till late into the night. Every room, bulging at the seams with guests and neighbours and the beaming proud parents welcoming them all with the doors to their hearts flung wide open. Even I could not contain this much joy and merriment. Dreamy, twinkling fairy lights were hung from every fruit tree in the garden. The folk songs sung by all the womenfolk echoed up the stairs into the very rafters and carried across the valley deep into the mountains.

Suddenly the *tumbaknari* missed a beat. And then another and within seconds, we realized, what was happening. The music drowned in the deafening sound of rapid bullets. There was a long pause. Silence! Only terrified breathing and the pounding of a hundred hearts. And then it was back! They hissed through the air and ricocheted off the walls. Windows shattered and the floors heaved under the weight and the dull thump of bodies hitting them. Heart-wrenching screams and an indiscriminate rain of hot lead were everywhere. Blood drenched the new carpets, people scurried like trapped rats while others just lay doubled over, their dead heads in their feast-filled plates. The poor little children suffered the most. Trampled to death! Sandals hitting and kicking tiny heads and ribs, their mothers shielding them desperately and even in death, their lifeless bodies like mountains giving cover. Old people wailed helplessly. The pot of henna shattered and all its contents mingled slowly with the blood of the groom. My sweet princess, my Heer lay on the floor in her shimmering baby blue *sharara*, lifeless like a rag doll, her hennaed hands clutching her own intestines, blood oozing out through her beautiful fair fingers. Death danced at the engagement for a full and long fifteen minutes that night. And then there was silence. No one was left alive to mourn. The same silence hangs in the air till today.

I was witness to all this but I could do nothing. I could not keep them out. My walls could not stop the guns. I can see those blood stains even today on my floor; I bear the holes and scars from every bullet that pierced through me, even today. I can hear those screams of horror every night and I live that nightmare alone every day.

I am the only survivor of that heinous night when men rode in, as devils in the name of their God.

Messengers of God!? Ha! Who is this brutal God that tells them to murder babies?

After they were done with the murder and mayhem, they summarily sat down to eat like one does after a long day at the office. Bodies, still warm lay all around them. But with not a shred of shame or remorse, they heaped their plates high and relished the feast that was not theirs to take.

I could do nothing. I could not offer any help! What could I do? I was only a home that had in one fateful evening turned into a graveyard. I am now just an empty shell, a carcass, with a few walls, and barely a roof. I am a weather-beaten, dilapidated structure, crumbling, sagging, and cracked like an old face full of regret. My gaping curtain-less windows look like dead hollow eyes where years of muddy rain have left streaming tear stains. I stand here alone just bones and bricks and curling timbre. And nurse the deep ache in my soul. It happened years ago but the wound feels fresh. I keep picking on the scabs, can't help it. How can I still be here when they are all gone? Why don't the vines and creepers pierce me with their tentacles faster and bring me down? I want to lie down and become one with the ground. The branches of the brazen mulberry tree are already inside the living room and the roots of the wild ones have been burrowing deep into the darkness, attacking my very foundation. Oh, be done with it. Grow faster, why don't you?! Please! I can't take it anymore.

I may be alone but I know I am not the only one. There are countless dead houses that were once homes full of life. Not only in Kashmir but in Afghanistan, Sudan, Syria, Iraq, Ukraine, Manipur, and Gaza… so many places, so many homes. If not ravaged by hate and greed then destroyed by the elements. All the love that once lived there is now replaced with vengeance or hurriedly packed into suitcases to flee. So many homes abandoned and like me, barely standing, in their own wreckage and rubble, waiting.

But wait we must. And as impossible a dream as it may seem, hope we must. Hope and pray that after all the springs, summers, autumns, and winters, a fifth season shall arrive, a season of peace and trust and kindness and tolerance. I know you think me silly. But I have nothing else left. The only thing that keeps me standing is this faint hope that someday this season will come. And some day another sweet gentle little Heer will squeal and run from room to room as she chases her brothers. Some day my cold hearth will be alive again and my chimney will be smoking into the air Some day…

* * * * * * *

www.ingramcontent.com/pod-product-compliance
Lightning Source LLC
Chambersburg PA
CBHW020021260726
48782CB00024B/168

9798892337748